'ERRANCE DICKS

# THE
# BOMBAY
# DEATHS
# INCIDENT

Piccadilly Press • London

D1395986

202254
Au

First published in Great Britain in 2001
by Piccadilly Press Ltd.,
5 Castle Road, London NW1 8PR

A catalogue record for this book is available from
the British Library

ISBN: 1 85340 725 9 (trade paperback)

1 3 5 7 9 10 8 6 4 2

Printed and bound in Great Britain by Bookmarque Ltd.

Cover design by Judith Robertson
Set in 12pt Palatino

*Terrance Dicks* lives in North London.
He has written many books for Piccadilly Press including the
CHANGING UNIVERSE series and the SECOND SIGHT series.

# PROLOGUE

*The minister raised his head from the pile of papers on his desk and yawned wearily. He rose and stretched, gazing abstractedly around the old-fashioned, luxurious study. It hadn't changed since the days when the British still ruled India.*

*There were leather-covered sofas and deep armchairs. The mounted heads of tigers, boars and buffalo decorated the walls, and there were tiger skin rugs on the polished floor. French windows with draped velvet curtains gave on to an exotic garden filled with colourful tropical plants.*

*The minister picked up a square of brightly-coloured glossy card, studied it for a moment, then spun it contemptuously behind him towards the French windows.*

*He turned back to his papers.*

*Silently, a man appeared behind him. He was an ordinary-looking young man wearing a high-collared* white cotton jacket and loose white trousers. The corner of a folded handkerchief peeped out from beneath the sash round his waist.

The minister tensed, somehow sensing the presence behind him. He straightened up and began to turn. He didn't live to complete the movement.

Leaping forward, the young man whisked the twisted handkerchief from beneath his sash, flinging it like a rope round the minister's neck. His knee went up into the minister's back and the hands holding the rope of cloth snapped sideways and back with tremendous force. There was the audible crack of a breaking neck . . .

The minister's body slid silently to the ground.

The killer took the twisted handkerchief from round the minister's neck. He looked down at the body. The minister lay on his back, head lolling horribly to one side, eyes staring wide in amazement.

The killer stood quite still, head bowed. Then he simply faded away. One minute he was there, the next he was gone . . .

## Chapter One

# GATEWAY OF INDIA

*I was in a temple. It was a terrifying place, vast and shadowy with ornately carved pillars. Torches blazed before the altar of a savage goddess . . . She was many-armed and she wore a necklace of skulls.*

*A giant snake weaved and writhed before the altar. It was enormous, far bigger than any known snake in the natural world.*

*Blood dripped from long, pointed fangs and the forked tongue flickered evilly.*

*Suddenly the massive head darted towards me . . .*

*I screamed – and woke up.*

Greatly relieved, I found I wasn't in a sinister Eastern temple, but in my hotel bedroom in Bombay. I sat up and tried to relax, thankful to see streaks of dawn light through a gap in the curtains.

I'd had several of these snake dreams since we'd been in India, and they seemed to be getting worse.

5

Maybe all the local colour was going to my head.

It took me a while to get back to sleep. When I did I overslept, and got told off by Dad for being late for breakfast . . .

We were admiring the Gateway of India when the police picked us up. We being me, Matt Stirling, and my father Professor James Stirling, all-round space boffin and general egghead.

We were in Bombay as a sort of side-trip. Dad had been attending a scientific conference in Australia, taking me along with him. He'd decided to stop off in Bombay on the way back. This was partly to improve my education – 'Everybody ought to see India at least once,' – and partly because he wanted to meet with a famous Indian computer scientist, who was working on a new system of computer guidance for space rockets. The man he wanted to see was away for a few days, and we were filling in time seeing the sights of Bombay. We'd started with the Gateway of India, which was right next to our hotel, the Taj Mahal.

The Gateway itself is a massive, ornately-decorated, triple arched affair in yellow stone on the shore of Bombay harbour. It was built in 1911 to celebrate King George the Fifth's visit to India.

Even though it's now an out-of-date monument to the vanished British rule, the people of Bombay are quite fond of the Gateway. They treat it as a symbol of their city, and the big open area around it is packed with peddlers, balloon sellers, snack sellers, snake charmers, anybody and everybody in Bombay with time to spare for a seafront stroll. Including, of course, the beggars.

I was used to beggars in England, but Bombay beggars were something else. There's not much of a social security system in India so if you're broke and out of work – and plenty of people are – it's beg or starve. Quite a few Bombay beggars look as if starvation isn't very far away. They come in all ages, shapes and sizes and they never stop coming.

Dad told me how to cope with the beggars the first day we arrived.

'Fill your pockets with small coins every morning, all you can afford, and hand them out to the first-comers until they're all gone. It's not much, but it's all you can do.'

'So, what do you think of Bombay?' asked Dad now, as I handed my last few coins to a hungry-looking girl clutching a baby.

'It's too much,' I said.

Dad frowned. 'Proper English, please, Matthew.

7

You know I dislike sloppy teenage slang!'

'I wasn't using slang,' I said. 'I meant exactly what I said. Bombay's too much. It's too hot, too crowded, too noisy, too polluted, too rich, too poor, too ugly and too beautiful. Too much of everything!'

He nodded gravely. 'India can be overwhelming. But it's a wonderful country all the same. And Bombay is a wonderful city.' He made a sweeping gesture towards the noisy chattering crowd all around us – nearly braining the nearest beggar, a scrawny old man, who ducked just in time and began showering us with what were presumably curses. Dad gave him a few coins, the curses changed to what sounded like blessings and the old man hobbled away.

'Just look at all these people,' Dad went on. 'Lots of them are just surviving from day to day, but they still carry on, hoping things will get better.'

There was the sudden blaring of a car horn, and a black car drove towards us, scattering the crowds. There were shaken fists and angry yells – which died away when the car pulled up beside us and two figures jumped out. They wore crisply-pressed khaki uniforms and forage-caps and carried long thick bamboo canes. For a moment I thought they were soldiers, then realised they must be police.

Both men looked alike, hard-faced types with neatly-trimmed black moustaches. The one who seemed to be in charge marched up to Dad.

'You are Professor James Stirling?' he said in clipped, slightly sing-song English.

'I am.'

'You are coming with me, please.'

Dad hates being given orders. 'Oh, am I? Why?'

'Orders,' said the policeman.

'Whose orders?' demanded Dad.

'Inspector *sahib* is wishing to see you urgently.'

'Well, maybe I don't wish to see him!'

Someone in the crowd shouted a jeering remark, and the policeman scowled angrily.

'It is not a matter of what you are wishing! Inspector *sahib* has ordered you be brought before him.' Angrily he slapped the cane against his leg. *'So get in the car, professor – now!'*

## Chapter Two

# DA SOUZA

Dad turned an alarming shade of purple. He opened his mouth and drew in a deep breath, obviously about to give the policeman a thorough blasting – one that would very likely end in our arrest.

Before he could get started, I intervened.

'Excuse me.'

The policeman swung round on me irritably. 'Well, boy?'

'I'm Matthew Stirling, Professor Stirling's son. My father's a leading scientist, a very important man. He has many influential friends in Bombay.'

The policeman gave me a worried look.

'What are your orders?' I asked.

'To find Professor Stirling and bring him to see Inspector Da Souza, as a matter of urgency.'

'You weren't told to arrest him, that he was wanted for some crime?'

The policeman didn't reply.

'So this is simply a request?' I persisted. 'You are *asking* him to come and see the inspector?'

The policeman drew a deep breath and turned back to Dad. He even saluted. 'Professor *sahib*, Inspector Da Souza requests as matter of importance that you will come to see him immediately.'

Dad looked at me and I nodded urgently. It was *almost* an apology – and it was the closest we were going to get.

With his dignity soothed, Dad said, 'Well, that's a different matter.' He got into the back seat of the car.

I followed him in, the policemen jumped in the front, and the car sped away, scattering the crowds with the blaring of its horn.

The blaring continued as we turned into the almost permanently gridlocked Bombay traffic. Some cars gave way, most ignored the horn altogether. Slowly we forced our way through.

Eventually we turned off into quieter streets, lined with more prosperous-looking houses. We began to climb.

As we sped along Dad turned to me and said, 'What do you think this is all about, Matthew?'

I shrugged. 'No idea. Maybe it's connected to your job.'

When funding for Dad's space research dried up,

he was offered the post of Director of Paranormal Studies for a big American science foundation. It wasn't exactly his line, but they needed a big-name scientist to head the project. What's more, they offered a generous salary and unlimited expenses. Reluctantly, Dad took the job.

Even more reluctantly he'd accepted responsibility for me, the fifteen-year-old son he hadn't seen since I was a baby.

(Mum and Dad split up soon after I was born. Mum brought me up alone and, when she died in a car accident, I was farmed out to an uncle and aunt. When they retired and went to live abroad, they passed me smartly back to Dad.)

Dad took over my education and took me on as his assistant. We'd survived a series of dangerous adventures together, getting to know each other in the process. Things were still a bit tricky sometimes, but we got along surprisingly well.

We turned into a steeply-rising street and stopped before a modest-looking house, set back from the road. The policeman got out and led us up the front steps and into a cool dark hall.

Dad looked round suspiciously. 'This isn't a police station!'

'This is the private residence of Inspector Da

Souza,' said the policeman. 'He is wishing to see you in circumstances of utmost discretion. Wait here, please.'

He went down the hallway, tapped at a door at the end, opened it and went inside.

Dad gave me another worried look. 'What do you think, Matthew? Are we being arrested – or kidnapped?'

'Neither, I hope. Look on the bright side, Dad. If this Da Souza's had us brought to his private house, he's hardly going to chuck us in a cell.'

The policeman returned and said, 'Come this way, please.' He led us to the room at the end of the hall and showed us inside.

We found ourselves in a small, simply-furnished study. It held a desk with a computer, bookshelves and a scattering of chairs.

Behind the desk a tall, dark-haired man was getting to his feet. He wore a well-cut dark suit in some lightweight material, with a white shirt and a striped regimental-looking tie. He had handsome features and a thin moustache.

'Professor Stirling? It is a very great honour to meet you. Allow me to introduce myself. I am Inspector Da Souza of the Criminal Division. It was extremely kind of you to agree to come and see me.'

'We were given very little choice,' said Dad grumpily.

Da Souza frowned at the policeman, who was standing rigidly to attention by the door.

'I trust there was no discourtesy? If you have any complaint . . .'

The policeman looked alarmed – and I looked hard at Dad.

'No, no,' he said grudgingly. 'Your officer was extremely keen to impress us with the urgency of the situation.'

The policeman looked relieved.

Inspector Da Souza dismissed the policeman and looked enquiringly at me.

'This is my son Matthew,' said Dad. 'He is also my assistant, and he is in my complete confidence.'

'As you say, professor,' said Da Souza. 'Please, be seated.'

We sat. 'Now then,' said Dad impatiently. 'What can we do for you?'

Da Souza paused. 'It is hard to know where to begin. There has been a series of most appalling crimes . . .'

'My dear man, we're not detectives,' interrupted Dad.

'Give the inspector a chance to explain, Dad,' I

14

said. 'I don't suppose he expects us to help cut down the number of burglaries in Bombay.'

Da Souza gave me a grateful look. 'No indeed. The crimes I speak of are murders, a string of brutal murders.'

'All the same,' said Dad obstinately. 'Murder, or any other crime come to that, is outside my field. We specialise in the paranormal.'

'Precisely!' said Da Souza. 'These murders have a strong paranormal element. I had heard of your work and when I learned you were in Bombay, I decided to ask for your help.'

Dad frowned. 'With respect, inspector, Bombay is a big modern city and you're bound to have your share of crime. Are these murders really so different, so important?'

'Very much so,' said Da Souza. 'If they're not stopped, and stopped soon, the whole city may well go up in flames.'

*Chapter Three*

# THUG

Dad frowned. He has a very British dislike of exaggeration, and a strong suspicion that all foreigners tend to get hysterical given the slightest encouragement.

'Isn't that rather melodramatic?'

'It's the literal truth,' said Da Souza soberly. 'Permit me to explain.'

He paused for a moment, gathering his thoughts. 'The victims of these murders are all VIPs of some kind. Politicians, religious leaders, business tycoons, film stars, sportsmen . . . All important, most of them popular and influential as well.'

'Do they have anything else in common?' asked Dad.

'It is more a question of their differences,' said Da Souza.

'How do you mean?'

'We have many races and religions here in

Bombay. Hindus, Muslims, Sikhs, Parsees, Anglo-Indians like myself, and a sizeable European community. The victims are drawn from all of them.' He paused. 'Some of these groups have a history of mutual hatred and suspicion. As recently as the early nineties there were terrible riots here in Bombay. Thousands of people died. Things are calmer now, but the old feelings are still there under the surface.'

'The murders are stirring up racial and religious tension?'

'Already there have been riots. Minor ones so far. But if this goes on . . .'

'I can see the crimes have a political dimension,' said Dad. 'But where does the paranormal come in?'

Da Souza frowned. 'Perhaps paranormal isn't precisely the right word. But there is certainly something very strange, almost uncanny, about these killings.'

'What exactly?' snapped Dad.

'All the victims died of a broken neck – snapped from behind with tremendous force.' Da Souza paused. 'It was the method used by the Thugs. Are you familiar with Thuggee, professor?'

Dad likes to think he's familiar with everything.

'An ancient murder cult of some kind, wasn't it?

Surely it died out years ago?'

'So we thought,' said Da Souza.

As it happened, I was familiar with Thuggee as well. My information came from an old movie on telly called, curiously enough, *The Stranglers of Bombay*. I didn't say anything about it, though. I think my late-night telly viewing is very educational, but Dad doesn't approve.

'The Thugs flourished over two hundred years ago,' Da Souza went on. 'They worshipped Kali, the most savage and cruel of the many Indian gods and goddesses. The Thugs believed, quite sincerely, that Kali had given them all travellers as their rightful prey. They were also known as the Deceivers.'

'Why?' I asked.

'Probably because of the way they operated. In the days before trains and cars, people travelled all over India on foot. For fear of robbers and bandits, the wealthier ones travelled in groups, with servants and armed guards. The Thugs would disguise themselves as a group of humble travellers and go on the road. They would track down some wealthy traveller, a maharaja or a prosperous merchant, and beg to be allowed to join his party for the night and share the protection of his guards.'

Da Souza stared into space as if seeing some

distant horrible scene. Then he went on. 'Sometime during the night, the Thugs would spring on their fellow travellers and murder them – all of them. They always used the same weapon, the one decreed by Kali.'

'Some kind of scarf, wasn't it?' I asked, remembering my old movie.

Da Souza nodded. 'A three foot square of cloth, twisted diagonally into a rope. It was called a *rumal*. They'd wear it tucked into a sash or a loincloth, with just one end peeping out. They tied a coin into the other end, to make it swing more easily. At a given signal they'd spring on their chosen victim from behind, loop the scarf around his neck, and then . . .' He paused. 'I say "he", but the Thugs murdered women and children as well. *Everybody*. No one was left alive to tell of the Thugs' existence.'

It was a ghastly picture, I thought.

Weary travellers sitting around a campfire, eating and drinking, talking over the events of the day. Then, at the given signal, the humble newcomers becoming murderous Thugs, springing on their victims, the deadly *rumals* swinging silently in the darkness. Strangled cries and the crack of breaking necks in some jungle clearing . . .

'When their victims were dead they robbed them,'

Da Souza went on. 'The bodies were stripped of money, jewels, anything of value. Then they dug a mass grave, a giant pit, and buried them. Afterwards, the Thugs scattered, each returning to their towns and villages, becoming respectable citizens again.'

Dad was becoming fascinated almost in spite of himself. 'How long did this disgraceful business go on?' he asked.

Da Souza shrugged. 'For hundreds of years. The Thugs are reckoned to have murdered over a million travellers in their time.'

'And they're still doing it?' I asked.

'I don't believe the people responsible for these murders are really Thugs,' said Da Souza angrily. 'However perverted, Thuggee was a genuine religion. The Thugs believed Kali had given them the right to prey on travellers. They never killed at home, only on the road. And they always killed for profit, following the rituals laid down by the goddess.'

Dad shrugged. 'Clearly there's been some sort of Thuggee revival, a degenerate form of the original cult.' He stood up. 'I'm sorry, I really don't see how I can help you, inspector. I fully realise the seriousness of the problem, but it simply doesn't fall into our area.'

'I think it does,' said Da Souza. 'As I told you,

the murders have one other thing in common – a paranormal element.'

'In what way?'

'They are all impossible murders.'

Reluctantly Dad sat down again. 'Go on.'

'Bombay has always been a dangerous city. It's quite usual for wealthy and important people to have bodyguards. Since this wave of murders, it has become universal. *All* the victims had excellent security – but they were killed just the same.'

'Every security system has flaws,' said Dad obstinately.

'Take the latest victim,' Da Souza went on. 'A government minister, head of a special commission investigating corruption in the film industry. It was felt that his life might be in danger from the villains he was investigating. He was provided with an armed guard. Last night the minister was found dead in his study, his neck snapped like all the others. But the villa where he lived was *sealed*. It was impossible for any intruder to get in or out. But the minister is dead all the same. He was found dead in his study, in a villa surrounded by troops. No trace of the murderer was found, in this latest case or in any of the others.' He looked appealingly at Dad. 'Not just one but a whole string of impossible murders, Professor Stirling. Surely paranormal forces must be involved? Won't you at least make a preliminary investigation?'

Dad nodded thoughtfully. He turned to me. 'What do you think, Matthew?' He can be surprisingly good sometimes about counting me in.

'I think we should take a look,' I said. 'We've got to stay in Bombay until your computer boffin gets back. We might as well try and make ourselves useful while we're here. And if there's any chance at all that we can help to prevent more riots . . .'

That did it. You can always get Dad by appealing to his sense of duty. Even if the British Empire had given up on Bombay and its problems, *he* wasn't going to . . .

'Very well, inspector,' he said. 'I shall only be in Bombay for a few more days, but if there is anything I can do in that time . . . In a purely advisory capacity, of course.'

Da Souza beamed. 'I am most grateful to you, professor. All the relevant files will be made available to you. Meanwhile, shall we visit the scene of the latest crime?'

'Very well.'

'I shall arrange for a car at once,' said Da Souza, and hurried from the room.

Dad gave me one of his cynical looks. 'Well, I hope you're satisfied, Matthew!'

Strangely enough, I was! I don't know why I was so keen to get involved – a mixture of reasons, I think.

I liked Da Souza and I felt curious about this series of impossible murders, with their mysterious and exotic background of Thuggee. Maybe I'd never got over that old *The Stranglers of Bombay* movie. And to be honest, I'm not really a keen tourist. This seemed a lot more interesting way of spending my time in Bombay than trailing round monuments and museums with Dad in the muggy heat.

But there was something else . . .

Something to do with the giant snake that haunted my dreams . . .

*Chapter Four*

# DEATH IN A GARDEN

When we arrived at the gates of the late minister's villa, an armed sentry barred our way. The sentry was young and nervous and it took a lot of angry shouting and waving of his police pass by Da Souza to get us through.

'Military idiot,' muttered Da Souza as we drove up the drive.

'Why are the soldiers still here?' asked Dad. 'If the poor man's dead . . .'

'He died only last night,' said Da Souza. 'The villa is still a crime scene. My men have been searching to see if the murderers have left some clue.' He sighed. 'Not that they ever do.'

He led us up the steps and a handsome, immacu-lately-uniformed young Indian Army officer appeared in the open doorway.

'Da Souza, my dear fellow!' he cried. 'How awfully nice to see you again!'

'This is Lieutenant Mohan, in charge of the guard detail,' said Da Souza. 'He did his officer-training at your British Sandhurst,' he added dryly.

'Best time of my life,' said the lieutenant enthusiastically. 'Bunch of damn fine fellows.'

'This is Professor Stirling,' Da Souza went on, 'and this is his son, Matthew Stirling. They are acting as consultants in this investigation.'

Mohan gave me a friendly nod and turned to my father. 'Honoured to meet you, Professor Stirling. Heard one of your lectures at Sandhurst. "Space and War." Didn't know this sort of thing was in your line.'

'Professor Stirling is also an expert on the paranormal,' said Inspector Da Souza. 'He is going to help us with some of the more baffling aspects of these cases.'

'Baffling's the word,' agreed Mohan. 'Whoever got in here and polished off the poor old minister – and got away afterwards – must have been a ghost, or a demon. No ordinary human could have managed it.'

'You're sure of that?' asked Dad sharply.

'Positive. The whole place was under guard, front and back, day and night. My lads are mostly raw recruits but they're dead keen, *and* I was up all night checking up on them.'

'Maybe the killers were some kind of Indian ninja,' I suggested.

Everyone stared at me.

'Legendary Japanese warriors and assassins,' I explained. 'They had some mystic power of making themselves unnoticeable. They could walk right past a sentry, or stand in the corner of a crowded room and you just wouldn't see them.'

Dad sniffed. 'A little fanciful even for you, Matthew.'

'Come and take a look at the scene of the crime,' said Mohan. He led us inside the house, across the hallway and into a spacious, old-fashioned study.

Three plainclothes detectives were searching the room. One of them, a plump, cheerful-looking character, looked up when we came in and hurried over to us.

'This is Sergeant Ganesh,' said Da Souza, and introduced us. 'Any luck, sergeant?'

Ganesh shook his head. 'Nothing, inspector *sahib*.' He nodded towards the desk. 'Over there are many dossiers and documents concerning corruption in film world, but papers do not appear to have been disturbed.'

Da Souza frowned. 'Strange.' He turned to Dad. 'Originally we suspected the Mumbai Mafia might be responsible for this murder. But they would have taken the papers in the hope of slowing down the investigation.'

'What's the Mumbai Mafia?' I asked.

'Mumbai is now official name of Bombay,' explained Ganesh. 'Changed by order of the State. Since then we are calling local organised crime syndicates the Mumbai Mafia.'

'Well, it's got a certain ring to it,' I said.

'Maybe they took some papers and not others,' suggested Dad. 'How incriminating are the ones that are left?'

They all went over to the desk and began examining the papers. I watched them for a while, got bored and began wandering around the room.

There was a chalk outline on the carpet in the shape of a sprawled-out body – something I thought only happened in old crime movies. The outline was between the desk and the curtains, closer to the desk.

I went over to the open French windows and examined the long drapes. Perhaps that was where the murderer had hidden. In which case he'd probably come in through the garden.

I pulled back the curtains. There was plenty of space for a man to hide. Moving the curtains revealed a square of brightly-coloured glossy card on the floor. I picked it up. It showed an impossibly handsome young man and an incredibly beautiful girl, gazing soulfully at each other against a montage of crashing helicopters, sports cars speeding down mountain roads and furious gun battles. The picture was overprinted with ornate lettering in Hindi. Perhaps it was a clue . . .

I looked at the group by the desk, but they were deep in discussion over the papers and I didn't want to interrupt. Deciding to tell them later, I shoved the card into my pocket and went through the French windows into the garden.

Whatever Lieutenant Mohan said, I was convinced the assassin, or assassins, had managed to get in this way. It wouldn't have been too difficult. The big garden was a jungle of thickly-growing bushes, plants and flowers, threaded with narrow paths. There was plenty of cover. Surely a ninja-style assassin would have been able to elude a group of nervous young sentries?

I heard a sudden hoarse cry. '*Sahib*, look out!'

I spun round and saw a man who'd appeared from nowhere. Something swished towards me. I ducked, and the something whispered over my head. To my horror I realised it was a long rope of cloth. It was a *rumal*, the weapon of the Thugs.

A Thug had just tried to break my neck!

The man caught the free end of the *rumal* in his other hand and sidled towards me. He was dressed in white and his eyes were wide and blank. He looked as if he was drugged or hypnotised. He looked like a zombie – but there was nothing zombie-like about the speed with which he moved.

I think I was too scared to scream.

I backed away so he couldn't get behind me.

The Thug moved around in a circle, and I circled the other way, keeping us face to face. Could you be strangled from the front? Very likely – he'd just snap my neck in another direction!

If he got too close I was as good as dead . . .

We moved around each other in a sort of weird dance. I could see the Thug preparing to spring . . .

Suddenly a second man appeared from the bushes – presumably the man who'd shouted the warning. Dressed like the first, he was much smaller, almost a dwarf, with a hunched back and abnormally broad shoulders. Something flashed through the air, there was a crack and the Thug jerked backwards and fell. He twitched, just once, and then lay still.

The killer spat on the body and muttered some kind of curse. I backed away, wondering if I was next. But, astonishingly, the man tucked his *rumal* back in his sash, put his palms together and bowed. Then he stepped back into the bushes and vanished.

My voice came back then. I stood in the peaceful garden, a dead Thug at my feet, and bellowed 'Help! Help! Murder!' at the top of my voice.

A young soldier came running down the path. He skidded to a halt at the sight of the dead Thug, then turned and ran back, shouting something in Hindi.

Moments later Dad, Lieutenant Mohan, Inspector Da Souza and several more soldiers came thundering down the path from the house.

Dad reached me first. He looked down at the dead Thug in unbelieving horror.

'Are you all right, Matthew? What happened?'

I drew a deep, shuddering breath, tried to stop shaking, and did my best to tell him. Before I finished speaking, Mohan was shouting orders to his men. They scattered and he went after them. I heard them pounding along the gravel paths and crashing through the bushes as they searched the grounds.

When I'd finished my story Dad said, 'He didn't hurt you? You're all right?'

'I'm fine,' I said, a little shakily. Being nearly murdered yourself, and seeing someone else killed under your nose, has quite an effect on the nerves.

Dad turned angrily to Da Souza. 'So this villa is

still a crime scene, sealed and under guard? Yet not one but two Thugs can stroll calmly in here and threaten the life of my son!'

'Be fair, Dad,' I said. I was starting to pull myself together by now. 'Only one of them threatened my life. The other one saved it.'

Lieutenant Mohan came back in time to hear the exchange. 'I understand your anger, sir,' he said. 'The fault is mine, I apologise. Your security was my responsibility. I have failed. I shall resign my commission.'

'I too apologise, professor,' said Da Souza. 'I was the one who led you into danger. And you, lieutenant, do not blame yourself, I am sure that you did your duty. We have been faced with such events in nearly all these murders – killers who seem able to evade the tightest security.' He turned to Dad. 'Remember, professor, it was *because* we were faced with the unexplained that we asked for your help.'

Reassured that I – and my neck – were both still in one piece, Dad was calming down. 'I'm the one who should apologise, gentlemen,' he said stiffly. 'The shock of realising what so nearly happened . . .'

'Did your men's search reveal anything, lieutenant?' asked Da Souza.

Mohan shook his head. He looked appealingly at Dad. 'I swear to you, professor, the villa is, and was, secure. There are sentries all round the perimeter, others covering the grounds, and still more inside the villa. Any intruder should have been detected and captured immediately. Yet . . .' He looked down at the dead Thug and shook his head in despair.

Da Souza knelt and made a swift search of the body. He straightened up. 'No identification, nothing. Please arrange for the body to be taken to the morgue, lieutenant.'

Mohan snapped an order and two men began carrying the body towards the gate. The head lolled hideously to one side. I shuddered and looked away.

'I suggest we return to the house,' said Da Souza.

As we went back up the path, one thought was filling my mind. Unpleasant as the attack had been, it was understandable. Somehow the Thugs had learned Dad and I were investigating the murders. We were a danger to them. By killing me, they hoped to get rid of Dad as well. Distraught with grief, he might well have given up and taken my body home.

Terrifying as the idea was, I understood why a Thug might want to kill me.

But why had another one turned up and saved my life?

*Chapter Five*

# INVITATION
# TO DANGER

I was still brooding about it as the police car carried me through the crowded and colourful streets of Bombay. Trying to distract myself, I stared out through the car window.

The traffic was terrible. Cars of every known make and in every condition, from gleaming Mercedes to battered old Fords, crawled slowly along the rutted and potholed roads.

Huge double-decker buses barged through the traffic jams like elephants, and bicycles and cycle-rickshaws darted through the gaps. There were even motorised rickshaws, odd-looking vehicles like three-wheeled mini-taxis. People were everywhere, flooding along the pavements, dodging between the slow-moving traffic. It was a varied crowd. Most of the men wore European dress, jeans or sports trousers and shirts ranging from sober white to gaudy Hawaiian. Some of the women wore Western dress as well, though many wore colourful saris.

There were priests in flowing robes, and holy men in loincloths, khaki-uniformed policemen trying vainly to control the traffic and the crowd. People chattered, shouted and argued, car horns blared, whistles blew and the oppressive, muggy heat bore down on everyone.

My combined driver and bodyguard, a cheerful young policeman called Darshan, shouted over his shoulder. 'How are you liking Bombay?'

'It's amazing,' I said truthfully. 'Is it always as busy as this, or have we hit the rush hour?'

'In Bombay it is always rush hour,' said Darshan.

'I don't know how you all stand it,' I said. 'To be honest, it's pretty exhausting.'

Darshan seemed more flattered than offended. 'That is true. You are needing to be tough to survive in Bombay.'

You're telling me! I thought, remembering what had happened in the garden . . .

After the murder we'd held a conference back in the study.

'What baffles me,' said Da Souza, 'is why one

Thug should attack you, and another kill *him* to save your life.'

'Perhaps there are factions,' suggested Dad. 'Extremists and moderates. One group was prepared to kill Matthew, the others felt that killing a child –' He saw my indignant expression and corrected himself, 'felt that killing someone so young was going too far.'

'Possibly,' said Da Souza. 'But it is hard to think of a gang of ruthless murderers having scruples about anything.'

I was inclined to agree with him. I remembered what he'd said earlier. *'The Thugs murdered women and children as well. Everybody. No one was left alive to tell of the Thugs' existence.'*

Whatever the reason my life had been saved, it hadn't been out of compassion.

'Perhaps the killing wasn't properly authorised,' Da Souza went on. 'I have heard that members of our Mumbai Mafia have been executed by their own chiefs for killing someone they hadn't been ordered to kill.'

'You said the second Thug muttered something, Matthew, after he killed your attacker,' Dad went on. 'Can you recall what it was?'

I tried to remember. 'It was a single word, like a

curse. He spat on the dead body and growled something . . .'

'Can you remember the sound?' asked De Souza urgently. 'It might provide a valuable clue.'

'I remember there was something odd about it,' I said slowly. 'It sounded like "Nasty". It struck me as a bit of an understatement in the circumstances.'

'Was it actually "Nasty"?' asked Dad. 'Or just something that sounded like it? A Hindi word, perhaps?'

I struggled to remember. 'It wasn't "Nasty" . . . The end was harder. More like "Nas*tee*".'

'Could it have been *Nastik*?' suggested Lieutenant Mohan.

'That's it!' I said. '*Nastik*! What does it mean?'

'It means blasphemer,' said Da Souza. 'Evil-doer. Someone who has offended against the gods.'

'Which brings us back to my original suggestion,' said Dad. 'Maybe the factions in the Thug cult are theological, the orthodox against the reformed.'

We thrashed it around for a while longer but didn't get any further.

The discussion moved on to what to do next. As usual, Dad took charge.

First he wanted to go through the minister's papers with Da Souza, in case there was any clue to the reasons for this particular death. After that he intended to go back to Da Souza's HQ and study the files on all the other murders, in the hope of finding some kind of pattern.

There didn't seem to be any place for me in all this and I wasn't surprised when Dad suggested I return to the hotel. He wanted me out of danger – but he was concerned for my safety when I was out of his sight.

'I'm afraid there's nothing but a lot of boring paperwork ahead, Matthew,' he said. 'You've had a shocking experience, and there's bound to be a reaction. Go back to the hotel and lie down. Order whatever you want from room service for lunch and have a good rest. I'll join you for dinner and tell you what I've learned – if anything!'

To his surprise – and obvious relief – I agreed.

'I expect you're right. There's nothing I can do here, and I do feel a bit tired.'

Dad turned to Da Souza. 'You'll arrange transport, inspector? And security? Perhaps you could spare one of your policemen to drive him back, and look after him at the hotel?'

'Constable Darshan will drive him back in a police car,' said Da Souza. 'You will like him, Matthew. He is a nice young fellow and his English is good. He will take care of you until he is relieved by another officer.' He nodded to Dad. 'I assure you, professor, there will be a guard on Matthew's room at all times.'

Like Dad, he sounded pleased to get rid of me.

I found it all a bit irritating. The kiddies were being tucked safely away so the grown-ups could get on with the serious work.

Still, I didn't have any real argument against it, and I did feel a bit tired. Reaction, I suppose. I'd encountered death and danger before, but never in so direct and brutal a fashion. Like I said, seeing somebody's neck snapped right under your nose shakes you up.


So, here I was in the car with Constable Darshan, on my way back to the comfort and safety of the Taj Mahal hotel.

We reached it at last and parked illegally right outside. In India, as in most countries, the police park where they like.

Darshan escorted me inside the hotel, had a long conversation with the manager, and then saw me up to my room.

'Well, thanks for looking after me,' I said. 'Goodbye.'

'Oh, it is not goodbye, Matthew,' said Darshan.

'Not yet. I shall remain on guard outside your room until I am relieved.'

'Come and guard me from inside in comfort,' I suggested. 'I'll get some cold drinks and we can watch telly.'

Darshan looked tempted, but he shook his head. 'My orders are to guard the door until further security arrangements are in place. Inspector Da Souza is most keen on strict obedience to orders.'

'OK,' I said. 'Suit yourself.'

I felt in my pockets for the room key. My fingers encountered a stiff square of glossy cardboard – the one I'd found in the minister's study. In all the excitement I'd forgotten about it. I passed it to Darshan.

'Can you tell me what this is?'

He studied it for a moment and then looked up. 'Where are you getting this? It is most precious!'

'So what is it?'

'It is special VIP invitation to première of latest movie by Salmalin Balin, famous producer.'

'When is this première?'

Darshan looked at the card. 'This very same day.'

'What time?'

'At six o'clock.'

'Where?'

'Empire Cinema on Mahatma Gandhi Road. Very

famous old Bombay cinema in art deco style, completely restored for première.'

I looked thoughtfully at the card. If the minister was investigating corruption in the film industry why had he been invited to the latest film première? Perhaps the card was a clue after all. It might be interesting to find out. A plan was forming in my mind . . .

'It is a great pity that you cannot go, Matthew,' Darshan went on.

'Why can't I go?'

'Orders,' said Darshan firmly. 'You are to remain in your room under guard.' He looked hopefully at me. 'However, if you are wishing to dispose of invitation, I myself am hoping to be relieved from duty before six . . .'

I took the card from his hand and found my room key. 'This invitation is evidence,' I said firmly. 'The only person I'm giving it to is Inspector Da Souza.' I opened the room door and added, rather meanly, 'Besides, if I can't go, neither can you!'

I went into the luxurious suite and stood looking at the card. I looked at my watch. It was still quite a while until six o'clock. I'd just have to bide my time.

I tossed the card on a table, got myself a Coke from the mini-bar and switched on the English language channel on TV – CNN as usual. I watched the rolling news till I got bored with it and turned it off.

I considered ordering some lunch and realised I wasn't a bit hungry.

I went into my bedroom, kicked off my trainers and lay on the bed. After a while I dozed off . . .

*I was in a temple. It was a terrifying place, vast and shadowy with ornately carved pillars. Torches blazed before the altar of a savage goddess . . .*

*The giant snake weaved and writhed before the altar. It was enormous, far bigger than any known snake in the natural world.*

*Blood dripped from long, pointed fangs and the forked tongue flickered evilly. The snake's bulging eyes stared hypnotically at me, rooting me to the spot.*

*I stood before the altar, unable to move. Even though I knew the soft-footed strangler was creeping up behind me, the* rumal *ready in his hands . . .*

I awoke with a start and sat up, wiping the sweat from my brow. No more sleep, I decided. Not with the snake and the strangler waiting for me in my dreams.

I had a shower, looked at my watch and picked up

the invitation card on the table. Time to go. I didn't want to be late for the big occasion.

I went to the wardrobe and changed into my 'smart' outfit – dark trousers, blazer, white shirt and striped tie, black shoes instead of trainers.

I left a note on the table for Dad.

*I found an invitation to a film première in the minister's study,* I wrote. *Maybe I can learn something. Come and pick me up after the première if you can. Empire Cinema on Mahatma Gandhi Road.*

I headed for the door – and remembered about Darshan. He'd never let me leave the hotel room. If he'd been relieved, he would have passed his orders on.

Then I remembered something else. There was a connecting door between Dad's room and mine.

I went through into Dad's room, opened his door a little and looked cautiously along the corridor. I was in luck. Another policeman, one I didn't know, and who obviously didn't know me, was guarding my door. I opened Dad's door, gave the policeman a friendly nod and strolled down the corridor, heading for the lifts.

I was on my way to the cinema.

And I was heading straight into danger . . .

*Chapter Six*

# BOLLYWOOD PREMIERE

I moved through the busy Bombay streets with a great feeling of freedom, of having got off the leash. To be honest, there were guilty feelings as well, under the surface. I knew I ought not to be doing this. Dad would be worried, Da Souza would probably be furious. On the other hand, where was the harm? The minister certainly didn't need his invitation any more. And if his death was connected to the Bollywood film industry, I might pick up some clue. I'd left Dad a note saying where I was going. If he was really worried he could always come and get me. Besides, they'd tried to leave me out of things, to tidy me away.

I'd show them.

Repressing my guilty feelings, I went on my way. I'd got a Bombay street map and directions to the cinema at the hotel reception, and I had plenty of time to enjoy the trip. The pavements, as always, were crowded, but the crowd seemed good-humoured enough. No one seemed to mind my white face and Western clothes.

I turned into a little street lined with food stalls and suddenly realised I'd missed lunch. I was starving.

I put together a meal by pointing to what I wanted and holding out a handful of coins. *'Bhelpuri, sahib?'* said the wrinkled old stall lady with a wide grin.

*Bhelpuri* turned out to be a mixture of noodles, rice, potatoes, onions, chillies and a variety of unknown herbs, all served in a big cone of thin cardboard. Delicious. Using the same methods, I obtained something called *pave bhaji*, an assortment of spiced vegetables served in a bun. I washed this all down with an iced yoghurt drink called *lassi* and went on my way.

Looking at my map and at my watch, I realised I was still some way from the cinema. I decided not to take any chances and hailed a passing cycle-rickshaw. Luckily the rickshaw man, a scrawny little bundle of muscle, spoke good English.

'Empire Cinema, Mahatma Gandhi Road, *sahib*? *Acha!*'

*Acha* is an all-purpose word meaning fine, OK, no problem.

I jumped in and we sped away.

I couldn't help feeling like some old colonial colonel as I sat perched up behind the rickshaw man. On the other hand, I was giving him a job, which he seemed pleased to get. He weaved in and out of the traffic at a terrific rate and, surprisingly soon, the Empire Cinema came in sight.

It was an amazing building somewhere between an *Arabian Nights* palace and a giant wedding cake. It was floodlit, and surrounded by a packed crowd.

Lined by blue-uniformed security guards, a lane through the crowd led up to a cordoned off space before the main entrance. As we arrived, a stretch limousine was depositing a handsome young man and a gorgeously dressed girl to the rapturous cheers of the crowd. The crowd surged eagerly forward, and the security men shoved them back. The limo moved on and the glamorous pair swept up the steps and disappeared inside the cinema.

This was obviously the VIP entrance.

My driver looked up at me and I waved him onward.

As we wheeled up the lane a roar of laughter came from the crowd. We stopped outside the cinema and I jumped down, thrusting a handful of notes into the rickshaw man's hand to salve my conscience. He gave me a huge grin of surprise and delight, and pedalled rapidly away.

Security men descended on me from all sides, clearly intending to give me the Bombay equivalent of the bum's rush.

I produced my VIP invitation and held it up, and they retreated, bowing.

Trying to look as dignified as possible, I went up the steps and into the cinema, followed by the cheers of the crowd.

The cinema foyer was vast and ornate, with marble floors, teak columns and crystal chandeliers. It was also crowded, so I felt a bit less conspicuous.

Still clutching my invitation, I followed the movement of the crowd, which seemed to consist entirely of the rich and beautiful, and found myself climbing a marble staircase at the far side of the foyer. At the top a beautiful sari-clad usherette took my invitation, and another showed me to an armchair-sized seat in the back row of the huge cinema. This was definitely VIP territory.

I sat back in the luxurious cushions, watching my fellow VIPs take their seats. I was half-expecting to be thrown out any minute, but although I got one or two curious glances, nobody bothered me.

There was a long, long wait before the film actually

started. There were lots of VIPs still to arrive, and the really big ones came fashionably late.

Eventually, at about half-past seven, the cinema darkened, the curtains drew back and the film began.

Even though it was in Hindi, I managed to follow the plot – more or less.

There was a rich and kindly businessman with a loving wife and three sons. The eldest was a fine upstanding character, the middle one a bit of a tearaway, and the youngest a dreamy poet.

There was a cruel and evil businessman with a good and beautiful daughter, who loved the good businessman's eldest son.

Her evil father opposed the marriage and framed the good businessman for some crime. The good businessman went to prison, his business ruined and his family broken up.

The young poet son denounced the bad business-man, got beaten up by hired thugs and died in his old mother's arms.

(I was told later that somebody *always* dies in his old mother's arms in Hindi films. It's a rule.)

The good man's eldest son becomes a policeman, the tearaway becomes a bandit. At first they fight, but eventually they join forces to prove their father's innocence and avenge their young brother.

At least, I think that's more or less it . . .

The story moved on, broken up by romantic duets, amazingly long dance sequences, car chases, gunfights, fist fights, love scenes – but no kissing – comedy scenes, dramatic scenes and subplots that baffled me completely.

I looked at my watch and saw we were only an hour or so into the film and the good guys were still in bad trouble. It was going to take them another couple of hours and another dozen dance sequences to sort everything out. I was considering slipping away – I was at the end of the back row, so it would have been easy enough – when a large hand descended on my shoulder. I realised I had left it too late.

A deep, husky voice whispered in my ear. 'You are coming with me, please.'

I looked over my shoulder and saw a giant of a man looming over me. He wore a Western-style suit that strained over his massive body.

'Come,' he said again.

There was no point in resisting, he could have picked me up with one hand. I got up and followed him from the auditorium.

I got a better look at him in the foyer outside. He

had a pockmarked face, a bristly crew cut, a rock-like jaw and enormous hands.

I looked up at him, speaking as calmly as I could manage. 'What can I do for you?'

'Mr Balin, the producer, is wishing to see you.'

The eyes of the watching usherettes widened at the great man's name.

'What for?' I asked.

'He is wishing to know why you are entering cinema with forged invitation.'

'You've got it all wrong,' I said. 'The invitation's genuine – it's me that's the forgery.'

My little joke fell flat. The giant simply said, 'Come,' and jerked a massive thumb.

I followed him along lushly-carpeted corridors until we reached a heavy brass-studded door. He knocked, and then ushered me into an office that was nearly as large, and just as luxuriously decorated, as the cinema. At the far side of the room, across acres of carpet, was a huge desk with a small computer terminal. Behind it sat a big round man with a bald head and horn-rimmed spectacles. He was smoking a big cigar.

Typecasting, I thought. Mr Balin could have played a big film producer in one of his own melodramas. Trying to look as confident as I could, I marched across the carpet until I stood before the desk.

'How do you do, Mr Balin?' I said politely. 'It's a great honour to meet you. Not watching your own première?'

He gave me a benevolent smile. 'I have seen this film many times, young fellow,' he said. 'Many hundreds of times! When the film is over I shall join all my famous and fashionable friends, and they will all tell me how wonderful the film is, and what a genius I am. But do you know whose opinion really matters?' He pointed downwards with his cigar. 'The little people in the cheapest seats, in the cinemas in the poorest districts. The ones who queue for hours and bring their meals with them. In the very poor districts they bring stoves and cook their food in the aisles. *They* will finally decide if this film runs for months or vanishes overnight.' Mr Balin leaned back and regarded me benignly. 'You are enjoying the film?'

'Very much,' I said. 'It certainly seems packed with incident. Something for everybody.'

Mr Balin's expression changed from benign to malignant with frightening speed. 'Now, to more serious matters. Some time ago, I sent a special VIP invitation to this première to an old friend of mine, a government minister. Today I hear the sad news that the minister is dead – murdered. Naturally, I wasn't expecting to see him tonight. But then –' Mr Balin held up an invitation, presumably the one I'd used. 'All VIP cards are numbered and recorded on the computer. When the cards are handed in, we check against the computer list to see who has actually arrived. You will understand my surprise when I discovered that the minister's card had been used.' He gave me a malevolent stare from behind the big glasses. 'You are wearing dead men's shoes, so to speak, young fellow. Or rather, you have been sitting in a dead man's chair. That is a very dangerous position. So – *where did you get that invitation?*'

I didn't reply.

'Would you rather discuss the matter with Jalil, my special bodyguard? He can be most persuasive.'

Behind me, I sensed the giant security guard moving closer. Once again the massive hand descended on my shoulder. This time it began to squeeze, hard enough to hurt . . .

*Chapter Seven*

# KIDNAP

Like the good guys in the movie I was in bad trouble. My only chance was to bluff my way out.

I wrenched my shoulder from Jalil's grasp and swung round to face him.

'Do you think I could have a chair?' I turned back to Mr Balin. 'Only it's a bit of a long story . . .'

There was a gleam of amusement behind Balin's big glasses. 'You heard our guest, Jalil. Bring him a chair. We must show our visiting *sahib* every courtesy.'

Jalil picked up a heavy chair in one hand, swung it through the air as if he was about to brain me with it, then dumped it behind me. Thankfully I sat down.

'What is your name, boy?' snapped Balin.

'Stirling. Matthew Stirling.'

'Why are you in Bombay?'

'I'm here on holiday with my father, Professor James Stirling. He's a famous scientist.'

'And where did you get the stolen ticket?'

I leaned forward, looking earnestly at the great man. I'd decided to tell the truth – well, a version of it anyway. 'Look, I'm sorry about using the invitation. I know it wasn't meant for me – but I knew the real owner had no more use for it.'

'Where did you get it?'

'In the minister's study, this morning.'

'What were you doing there?'

'My father took me there.'

Mr Balin sighed. 'What was *he* doing there?'

At this point I embroidered the truth a little. 'He's a criminal psychologist. He often helps the police at home. A police inspector called Da Souza discovered he was in Bombay, and consulted him about the minister's murder.'

'And the invitation?'

'I got bored with listening to Dad and Da Souza discuss the case and went for a walk in the garden. On the way out I found *that* . . .' I nodded towards the invitation on the desk. 'I know I should have handed it to the police, but . . .'

'Has your father made any progress with the investigation?'

I made myself sound bored and sulky. 'No idea, he never tells me anything about his work. I shouldn't think so.'

'Why not?'

'He didn't really want to help; he's here on holiday. He was sort of press-ganged into it by this Inspector Da Souza. He was just going through the motions.' I paused. 'Anyway, he packed me off back to the hotel, and I was going crazy with boredom. Then I remembered I had the invitation. Everyone had been telling me what a terrific film it was, so I decided to come – and here I am!'

He looked keenly at me. 'So, your father and the police don't know where you are?'

I looked innocently back at him. 'Oh yes, they do. I left Dad a note telling him where I was going. He's coming to pick me up.'

Mr Balin sat back behind his desk, considering, his face unreadable. He might be about to let me go – or be about to tell Jalil to wring my neck.

Suddenly he beamed. 'Ah well, no harm done. Just a boyish prank, eh?' He chuckled. 'When I was a poor urchin I often sneaked through the emergency exit in the cinema to see the film free. All you've done is the same thing on a grander scale!'

I stood up. 'Thank you for seeing it like that. I'll be on my way then.'

He waved the idea away. 'No, no, you must see the end of my film. There is still nearly an hour before it ends. That is what you came for, isn't it?'

I hesitated. 'I really ought to be getting back. Dad will be worried.'

'I will call my old friend Inspector Da Souza and tell him you are safely here watching my film,' he said reassuringly. 'He will inform your father.'

'You know the inspector?' I asked.

'I am co-operating with him, as I was with the unfortunate minister, on an enquiry into corruption in the film industry. Many bad men are involved. They demand protection money, kidnap film stars, blackmail producers. Most are afraid to speak out, but I, Salmalin Balin, am not afraid. I intend to put an end to this villainy.' He drew a deep breath and then calmed down. 'Now, enjoy the rest of the film. The climax is particularly brilliant. You are welcome to attend the VIP champagne reception afterwards if you wish.' He waved me away dismissively. Jalil opened the door. It seemed best to go.

Back in my luxurious seat I watched the film unfold, though I didn't take much of it in. It seemed as if Balin was one of the good guys after all. Or at least, not an out-and-out villain. He was probably just a powerful man protecting his own interests. He'd been a bit heavy with me at first, but perhaps that was understandable. If he'd been co-operating with the murdered minister, it wasn't surprising that my using the dead man's invitation had alarmed him. After all, the most likely person to be in possession of the murdered man's invitation was his killer!

And if he was helping the police and defying the Mumbai Mafia – well, no wonder he needed a bodyguard like Jalil.

That's what I told myself. All the same, I still had a strange feeling that, despite my luxurious sur-roundings, and my new VIP status, I was in real danger . . .

The real test, I decided, would be if Mr Balin let me go without any fuss after the movie – especially if he'd phoned Inspector Da Souza as promised.

After several more fights, car chases, love scenes and dance sequences the film wound its way to a happy ending. The villain was exposed, the good businessman was freed, the bandit son reformed and the villain's beautiful daughter ended up in the arms of the virtuous policeman. (Still no kissing though.)

The closing titles came up to riotous applause from the audience. It looked as if Mr Balin had another hit. Then I remembered what he'd said in the office. The opinion of this fashionable crowd didn't really matter. The little people would decide.

With the crowd still cheering, I slipped out of my seat and went into the foyer. Jalil was waiting for me.

'Well, I'll be on my way,' I said hopefully. 'I think I'll skip the VIP reception, if you don't mind. I'd sooner go outside and wait for my father. Did Mr Balin phone Inspector Da Souza, do you know?'

Jalil nodded impassively. He turned and led me down the marble staircase and across the main foyer.

It was dark when we got outside – or would have been if it wasn't for the floodlights. The crowd of adoring fans was bigger than ever. They'd waited patiently in the oppressive heat to see the stars go in. Now they were waiting to see them come out again.

A ring of blue-uniformed security guards cordoned off the big, open space in front of the cinema, so the stars could leave in their stretch limos without being breathed on by their humble fans.

Jalil led me to a spot at the edge of the cordon, quite close to the seething crowd.

'We wait here for your father.'

'Wouldn't we be better on the cinema steps? I don't want to miss him.'

'Steps too crowded soon, many people leaving. Better here.'

Maybe he was right.

Limos began arriving, and the beautiful people

started coming down the steps. Presumably these were the B-list celebs, the ones who hadn't been invited to the VIP reception. You could see they were really nobodies, their limos weren't even stretch. The crowd didn't care though, they cheered them just the same.

I kept looking anxiously around for signs of Dad. For all Mr Balin's recent benevolence, I wouldn't feel really safe until I was away from here.

Suddenly a police car drove up, parking on the far side of the open space.

I breathed a sigh of relief. I was safe.

Constable Darshan jumped out and opened the rear passenger door. Dad got out, and Inspector Da Souza got out the other side.

'Dad!' I yelled, waving frantically. 'Dad, over here!'

He heard me and started running across the floodlit open space. Da Souza and Darshan followed.

Suddenly the crowd erupted, just at the point where we were standing. Or rather, a *section* of the crowd erupted. They surged forward, breaking through the cordon of security men.

Some of them were just ordinary fans, carried forward by the crowd. But at the heart of the rush was a group of tough-looking men in grimy clothes. They looked exactly like the villain's henchmen in the movie and, like them, they carried clubs, knives and guns. All at once I was at the centre of a milling, fighting, shouting crowd.

One of the gangsters sprang forward and hit Jalil under the jaw. He must have been stronger than he looked, because Jalil staggered back and fell. He jumped up and aimed a wild blow at his attacker, roaring to the other security men for help.

The blue-uniformed security men abandoned their crowd-control line and tried to come to his aid. More of the crowd surged forward in their wake. Beyond the wildly-struggling group, I saw Dad fighting desperately to reach me.

Somebody grabbed me around the waist, pulling me away. I kicked hard at a bare shin and broke free. But not for long. Somebody grabbed one arm, some-body else grabbed the other. I found myself being dragged through the crowd, gripped on both sides, a big, hard, grimy hand clapped over my mouth.

The brawling crowd seemed to open before us, then close up behind, preventing pursuit. Struggling wildly, I was borne through the crowd to a corner where an old grey van stood waiting. Someone opened the rear doors and I was thrown inside. Heavy bodies piled in after me, the doors closed, and the van jerked into life and roared away.

*Chapter Eight*

# PRISONER

I lay flattened on to the floor of the van, held down by the feet of the men sitting on the benches that ran along either side. I could hardly move or breathe, let alone struggle. I curled myself tightly into a ball and waited for the journey to be over.

As near as I could guess, the trip seemed to take about an hour. We moved slowly at first, probably moving through traffic. Later on we sped up a little and I guessed we were leaving Bombay.

The men above me muttered amongst themselves in some guttural tongue. One of them laughed – they seemed to be pretty pleased with themselves.

The journey ended at last and the van came to a halt. The doors were opened and everybody piled out, dragging me out last. I immediately collapsed in an agony of cramp. My captors thought that was very funny. I was dragged to my feet, and hauled across a patch of muddy ground. The air was damp and salty, and I could hear the distant roar of the sea.

I was thrust into some kind of building, the door was slammed and somebody lit a lantern.

I looked around. I was in a hut, quite a solid building made of mud bricks. There was a pile of tattered netting in one corner and some broken fish crates and boxes in another. Grouped around me were the men who'd kidnapped me, half a dozen villainous-looking types in grimy white clothes.

They went through my pockets, took my money and shared it out. One of them, obviously the leader, stole my watch. He even stole my tie but he was welcome to that. Then he said grimly, 'Give no trouble and you will not be hurt. Annoy us and we kill you, bury your body in the mud. Many people are disappearing in Bombay.'

There didn't seem any point in arguing – or in asking questions either. I sat on the pile of nets in the corner and kept quiet.

I guessed that this lot were just the low-level labour force, possibly hired specially for the job. Any instructions about my fate would come down from their boss. There was one consolation, though. Presumably they hadn't been ordered to kill me, or they'd have done it by now.

My captors squatted down nearby in a semicircle

and began to talk. Soon the talk turned into a heated argument. Holding up his hand for silence, the leader produced a greasy pack of cards. Shuffling them he fanned them out and everyone took a card. They compared cards and soon there were broad grins on the faces of all except one, the youngest-looking. Judging by his disgusted expression he thought they'd cheated him. Judging by the sly looks on their faces they had.

Another bandit was looking pretty fed up as well, but he was older and seemed more resigned.

For a chilling moment I thought they might have been drawing lots to decide who was going to kill me. Instead the leader said, 'We leave. Come back soon. These men guard you. Give no trouble or they kill you.'

The young bandit scowled ferociously and produced an evil-looking knife and a rusty revolver, brandishing them threateningly at me. The others all roared with laughter at this fierce display – which made him angrier than ever. They all went out of the hut, leaving the three of us alone. We heard the roar of the van as they drove away.

The odds had gone down.

The two bandits talked briefly for a moment. Then the older one shrugged and went outside. Presumably they'd take turns, one inside, one out.

I studied the remaining guard carefully. He might be the youngest of the band but he was still a lot bigger and stronger than me. He was mean-looking too. I was sure he'd used the gun and knife before and wouldn't hesitate to use them again – on me.

All the same something had to be done. Somehow I just had to escape before the others came back. I looked round the hut for something to hit him with.

One of the broken crates perhaps, though they looked a bit flimsy. There must be something. If I could distract his attention somehow, get behind him with something heavy . . . There was still the one outside, but if I could take him by surprise, hide behind the door when he came in . . .

I gave the young bandit a friendly smile. 'Gone down to the pub and left you on guard, have they? Never mind, maybe they'll bring you back a drink.'

He glared at me and muttered something, probably the Hindi for 'belt up'.

There was a mild scuffling noise outside, a sharp crack like the sound of a breaking twig, then silence.

The young bandit called out something, panic in his voice.

Silence.

Grabbing the lantern in his left hand, he moved towards the door and opened it a little, peering through the crack. Drawing his revolver, he kicked the door open. He held the lantern high, making a pool of light that revealed a huddled shape. It was the older bandit, his head twisted to one side at a dreadful, unnatural angle.

Glaring wildly around him, the young bandit took a step further outside.

A squat, shadowy shape slipped behind him – the man from the garden. I saw the swing of the *rumal*.

'No!' I yelled. 'Don't kill him!'

My shout warned the young bandit and he jumped back, bumping into the dwarf and spoiling his aim. The bandit tore the *rumal* from his neck and raised his revolver. I tackled him from the side, knocking him to the ground. The dwarf twisted the revolver from his hand and slammed the barrel behind his ear. The bandit went limp, letting go of the lantern. Miraculously, it didn't go out.

Recovering his *rumal*, the dwarf looked indignantly at me. 'Why are you interfering? I am having a clean strike.'

I looked at the older bandit, then at the unconscious younger one. 'Isn't one death a night enough? Besides, he's hardly more than a juvenile delinquent.'

'You British are too soft,' grunted the dwarf. 'That is why you lost India. Help me get them inside.'

We dragged the living and the dead body into the hut, dumping them on the pile of nets. The dwarf looked at the unconscious bandit.

'Safer to kill him, *sahib*.' His hand moved towards the *rumal*.

'No!' I said firmly. 'Just tie him up.'

The dwarf ripped off sections of the net with incredibly strong hands and we twisted them into ropes, binding the young bandit's arms and legs.

I picked up the lantern. 'We'd better get going before the others come back.'

'They are low-class gangsters only,' said the dwarf contemptuously. 'They go to the village to drink; they are not returning for many hours.'

And the drinks are on me, I thought, remembering my stolen rupees.

'Still, you are right, *sahib*,' the dwarf went on. 'We must leave at once, we have far to go.'

'Hold on a minute,' I said. 'You saved my life in the garden, and now you've rescued me again. Don't think I'm not grateful, but – why are you helping me? Who are you? And where are we going?'

The dwarf put his hands together and made his curious little bow. 'I am helping you because I need *your* help, *sahib*. I am Hussein, last of the true Deceivers. I am taking you to the temple of Kali.'

*Chapter Nine*

# KALI'S TEMPLE

It was quite an answer. I stared at him, absolutely astonished.

Somehow I managed to get my brain back into gear.

'Look, what's going on here? Who's behind all these murders, and why?'

This time he didn't answer my questions, at least, not directly.

'I am needing to show you. Unless you are *seeing* you will not believe. Come!'

I hesitated for a moment. Where was I going – and who was I going with? Hussein was a self-confessed Thug – the last of the true Deceivers, he'd said. But he'd undoubtedly saved my life. And he was certainly against whoever was committing this string of murders.

What's that old saying? *My enemy's enemy is my friend.*

I followed him from the hut. What else could I do?

Once outside I stood looking around. Bright moonlight revealed that the hut stood close to the edge of the sea. Before me was a muddy beach and, beyond, a wide sweep of moonlit sea. The air was heavy with the smells of salt and fish, and scrubby green vegetation stretched along the shoreline.

There were more huts in the distance, and further on a scattering of lights – the fishing village where my kidnappers were spending *my* rupees.

'Come!' said Hussein again. He led me around the back of the hut to where an extraordinary vehicle was parked. It was an ancient version of one of the motorised rickshaws that I'd seen on the streets of Bombay. It was even more beat-up than most, and seemed to have extra pipes and plates bolted on.

'My motorised rickshaw,' said Hussein proudly. 'I am finding it on dump, and am rebuilding myself. It is most superior vehicle. I could not prevent your kidnap, but I am following the villains here in this.'

He bent over and fiddled with the engine of the contraption and after a while it started to throb. The throb rose to a low roar. Hussein straightened up.

'Please to jump in, *sahib*. Starting is most tricky part of operation.'

I jumped into the passenger seat and Hussein

climbed into the driver's place. He made some more adjustments to the engine and we roared away.

Once again it was a longish journey. I learned later I'd been taken about fifteen kilometres from the centre of Bombay. The extraordinary vehicle rattled slowly along the rutted roads. The driving lights were pretty feeble, but Hussein didn't seem to mind. It was well past midnight but thankfully the bright moonlight was still shining. After a long time the flat, marshy countryside gave way to a scattering of shabby, broken-down buildings. We'd reached the edges of Bombay. I was nearly home.

But Hussein didn't take me to the comfort and luxury of the Taj Mahal hotel, at least not yet. Instead he drove me to a part of Bombay I'd never seen before, and hoped never to see again.

We'd reached Bombay's famous slums. I'd heard of them, vaguely, but nothing had prepared me for the full horror. All around me were rows and rows of muddy, unpaved streets, lined with an astonishing collection of rickety, hand-built huts and shacks. Compared to these places, the mud-brick fisherman's hut I'd just left was a palace. Here and there ruined buildings towered over the sprawling huts.

I learned later that millions of people in Bombay lived in slums like these. No running water, no sanitation, no electricity, nothing. And those too poor to afford even a shack lived, and died, on the streets.

Hussein drove up to one of the ruins and stopped his engine. He jumped down and pulled back a section of tarpaulin, held down by bricks and a chunk of iron, revealing a space that must once have been a garage. I helped him to push the rickshaw inside and replace the tarpaulin.

'Is it safe here?' I whispered.

'Oh yes,' said Hussein. 'No one is stealing from me.'

I nodded. I could well imagine that local villains steered clear of the little man with big shoulders and big hands – and the end of the *rumal* peeping from his sash.

'Come,' said Hussein. 'We walk now, we must not be heard.'

We hurried through the ruined streets, seeing only the occasional white-clad figure in the distance. Rats scuttled out of our path. One, a big one, sat right in the middle of the street glaring at us, only moving at the last minute.

Confidently Hussein led the way forward, steering his way through streets of rickety shacks and the tangle of rubble. Clearly, he knew every nook and cranny of the ruins.

At last we came to a circle of open ground in front

of a pile of rubble that had once been a building. Incongruously, a black limousine was parked before the ruins. A giant figure sat motionless behind the wheel. A figure that seemed curiously familiar . . .

I was struck by the sheer arrogance of leaving an expensive car in a place like this. Clearly the owners had no fear that the car might be stolen, or that someone might report its presence to the police.

Nobody would dare.

We skirted around the limousine in a wide circle, keeping out of sight by using the ruined buildings for cover. Slipping through narrow openings, ducking in and out of ruined doorways, Hussein led me at last to a narrow gap on the other side of the rubble. He squeezed through it and I followed. I found myself going down a steep flight of steps and then along a dank, dark tunnel. It was wet and smelly and altogether disgusting. Hussein produced a battered torch to light our way. As we moved onwards its beam caught dark shapes scuttling at our feet, and eyes and teeth gleamed savagely out of the darkness.

Rats! I thought, and shuddered.

Suddenly Hussein stopped. He beckoned me towards him, and I stooped down so that he could whisper in my ear. 'Be careful, *sahib*, and tread only where I tread. There are many traps.'

'What kind of traps?'

For answer Hussein moved on a little further, then suddenly flattened himself against the tunnel wall. I did the same and waited.

Gripping my arm to keep his balance, Hussein leaned forward, stretched out one leg, stamped on a flagstone in the centre of the tunnel floor, and jumped back.

The flagstone fell away like an opening trapdoor, revealing a square black hole from which came a foul stench and the sound of running water.

'The lower sewers,' whispered Hussein. 'There is no way out.'

Slowly the flagstone rose back into place – I suppose there must have been some kind of counterweight.

We moved on until we came to a narrow recess in the side of the tunnel. Hussein shone his torch inside, revealing an odd-looking wooden framework. He dropped to the ground and crawled along the slimy floor of the tunnel. Reluctantly I did the same.

As we crawled past the niche there was a sudden vibration and a sharpened stake shot out of the recess, shattering against the far wall of the tunnel.

If we'd simply walked past, we'd have been human kebabs!

We got up and moved cautiously on.

Hussein demonstrated – and avoided – more traps as we moved on our way. Some were simple – more stakes set into the floors and wall of the tunnel. Hussein shone his torch on the sharpened tips. They were smeared with some kind of oily gum.

'Poison,' whispered Hussein. 'One scratch is causing agonising death.'

Others were more elaborate.

Failing to follow Hussein's lead closely enough, I stumbled over some kind of tripwire. There was a rumbling from overhead . . . Instantly Hussein whirled round and threw himself at me, knocking me over backwards. Great blocks of masonry crashed down on to the spot where I'd been standing.

Shaking, I scrambled to my feet. 'Who set all these traps?' I demanded.

'Those who blaspheme Kali's temple, to frighten off intruders. Many have died, and now nobody comes here – except me! I am too clever for them.'

'Why do they go to such lengths to keep people away?'

'You will see, *sahib*. Come!'

As we moved on, I realised I was afraid. Not so much of the traps, though they were bad enough. I had a powerful sensation of doom and dread – and it was a curiously familiar fear. One I'd encountered before . . .

Eventually a light gleamed ahead. Hussein put out his torch.

'We are very close, now. No more traps – but there will be guards.'

We moved forward even more cautiously.

The end of the tunnel opened out into a rocky cave, strewn with rubble. On the far side was an ornately-carved, half-ruined archway, illuminated by blazing torches set into the wall.

On either side of the archway stood an armed guard.

I studied them closely. Both were roughly-dressed with hard villainous faces. They didn't seem to be Thugs – there was no sign of the sash or the *rumal*. Instead each carried a machine-pistol, ready for use. They were hired gangsters, I decided, much like the ones who'd kidnapped me earlier.

I saw Hussein reach for his *rumal* and grabbed his arm, shaking my head. However villainous the guards were, I didn't want to hear their necks snap.

Besides, how could Hussein get close enough to use his *rumal*? They'd shoot him down as soon as they saw him.

Hussein pulled his arm free and bent down to

select a chunk of rubble. He tucked it into the centre of the *rumal*. Holding both ends of the scarf in one hand, he whirled it around over his head like a slingshot then released one end.

The chunk of rubble flew across the cave and struck the sentry on the left between the eyes. He dropped to the ground. Astonished, the second guard ran across to him, bending over to see what had happened.

Hussein bounded across the cave, his big fist rose and fell in a hammer blow, and the second guard collapsed across the body of the first.

I crossed the cave to join Hussein and we went through the arch.

My sensation of fear welled back, stronger than ever now.

We came out on to a half-ruined balcony, high in the side of an underground temple. It was the temple of my dreams. There were the ornately carved columns and the blazing torches. There was the statue of the savage, many-armed goddess, the goddess I now knew to be Kali, with her necklace of skulls.

And there was the giant snake of my dreams, rearing up before the altar, forked tongue flickering and blood dripping from its fangs. Huge and unnatural, it was no living creature. It was the personification of the evil force that had taken over Kali's temple.

I felt a sensation of sheer horror, overwhelming fear. Once again, it was a *familiar* horror – as if somehow I'd encountered the evil force behind the snake before . . .

Somehow I felt that the snake *knew* me. If it turned and looked at the balcony it would see that I was there. For the moment, however, its attention was distracted.

A bulky figure appeared from the shadows holding a slimmer, younger figure by the arm. The bulky man wore ceremonial robes and a hideous mask. The other was wearing the loose white jacket and trousers so common on the streets of Bombay.

There was a sash round his waist.

The big man pushed the other man forward and then stepped back into the shadows. The white-clad young man stood alone, the giant snake rearing above him. He didn't seem to be afraid, more like dazed or hypnotised.

A blazing circle of light formed about him. He stood motionless for a moment, then simply disappeared into its brightness, fading away into nothingness . . .

'What's happening? Where's he gone?' I whispered.

Hussein put his lips close to my ear. 'Somewhere

a rich and powerful man sits alone in a room. There are bodyguards outside the door, and more around the house. The rich man thinks he is safe. In moments he will be dead.'

So that's how it's done! I thought. Translocation!

Translocation – the ability to leave one point in space and reappear instantly at another. I'd heard of it before, particularly amongst South American shamans and the Aborigines of Australia, but to see it like this . . . I turned to ask Hussein more about it, but he put his finger to his lips.

We waited. Everything in the temple was silent. The snake weaved, the torches flickered . . . The young man reappeared in the circle of light, the *rumal* between his hands.

Somewhere, somebody was mysteriously and horribly dead.

The bulky, robed figure appeared from the shadows and led the young man away.

Hussein tapped my shoulder and we left the balcony. Stepping over the still-unconscious guards, we set off back down the tunnel.

The return journey was slightly less horrifying, since some of the traps had been sprung and there hadn't been time to re-set them. Hussein knew about the others – at least, most of them.

We were feeling our way along a particularly narrow, dank tunnel when suddenly a noose dropped from above, tightening about my neck and starting to haul me upwards. Struggling desperately, I managed to get a hand inside the noose before it could strangle me.

Hussein produced a fearsome-looking knife and managed to reach up to cut me free. Gasping and choking, rubbing my neck, desperately longing to reach fresh air, I followed Hussein down the dark, slimy tunnel, rats slithering about our feet.

Shaken as I was, I felt a sense of grim satisfaction. At least part of the mystery was solved . . .


'We Deceivers are flourishing when nobody is knowing about us,' said Hussein. 'But you British discovered our secrets in the days when you ruled India. Gradually we were hunted down.'

'But not completely wiped out, the way everyone believed?' I suggested.

Hussein smiled. 'Not completely, *sahib*.'

It was some time later and we were sitting in the motorised rickshaw's garage, which was also Hussein's home. He'd lit a lantern revealing a straw mattress in the corner and a few meagre possessions on wooden shelves. In this district, the place probably counted as a mansion. Hussein had brewed tea on a spirit stove, and we sipped it as we talked.

I'd insisted on a full explanation before going home. Hussein was doing his best to provide it. It was an amazing tale.

The cult of Thuggee had never completely died out. Through the years a few isolated bands of Deceivers had carried on the bad work of their murderous ancestors. Hussein's band – he was *Jemedar* or Chief, had been the last. One by one the other members of the band had been arrested or killed.

'Our time was over,' said Hussein sadly. 'And no wonder! Today the law is forbidding human sacrifice . . .' He sighed. 'Kali must have her sacrifice. Without it she abandoned us.'

He sounded like a traditionally-minded English vicar, complaining that church services were no longer in Latin.

Left alone, Hussein had been forced to give up Thuggee and become a rickshaw-driver. He had stayed on as unofficial caretaker of the temple, praying to Kali and carrying out the occasional sacrifice. Not human, I hoped – but I didn't ask.

Then the great snake had appeared in the temple, driving him away.

The giant snake, Hussein insisted, was *not* a

manifestation of Kali but the form assumed by some demon, some unknown alien power that had taken over the temple.

He was right about that, I thought.

Hussein knew every inch of the ruins and the sewer tunnels that led to the temple beneath. He had hidden, watched and waited.

To his horror he had seen young people brought to the temple, taught how to use the sacred *rumal* and dispatched to kill – just as I had seen tonight.

It wasn't the killing that horrified Hussein but the lack of proper ceremony. To him it was sheer blasphemy. Some alien power was perverting his religion.

'They are making no prayers to Kali. They are not observing sacred omens. They are not kneeling on sacred blanket or tasting sacred sugar. Nor are they killing only travellers, as Kali ordains. Always I am hoping Kali will appear and punish them.'

'Could she?' I asked. 'The evil force seems to be very strong.'

'Kali is the Goddess of Death and Destruction,' said Hussein confidently. 'She has great and terrible powers and the light from her eyes is death.' He sighed again. 'But Kali did not come. I fear that now the true Deceivers are no more, she is abandoning her temple.'

Once he realised the true horror of what was happening, Hussein determined to frustrate the blasphemers' plans. He, at least, would be true to the spirit of Kali. Even though she had abandoned him, he would not forsake her.

'I am learning that they plan to kill the minister, and am trying to save him. I failed, and am trapped a long time, hiding from soldiers in the garden. That is why I am there to save you when they send another assassin.'

'How did you get there in the first case?' I asked. 'Can you just appear and disappear, like that man in the temple?'

Hussein smiled. 'No, *sahib* – but I am very small and very cunning. I am crawling between the legs of those young soldiers and they are not seeing me. That is how I escaped after killing the one who tried to kill you.'

'Why did you do that?' I asked. 'Save me, I mean?'

'Your father is a great and wise man. Perhaps you are both helping me to destroy these blasphemers.'

A touching faith in our abilities, I thought. Dad would be pleased. I wished that I shared Hussein's confidence.

'What do you want me to do?' I asked.

Hussein leaned forward. 'Yesterday I captured

someone high in their councils. I strangled him, just a little, and said he could live if he told me the blasphemers' plans. He is telling me of special plans, terrible plans for tomorrow night.'

'What happened to him afterwards?' I asked.

'He died,' said Hussein simply.

I shuddered and passed hurriedly on. 'So what's going to happen tomorrow night?'

'They are planning to send out not one but dozens of assassins. There will be a massacre of leading figures in all political parties and religions. Rumours will be spread, charges and counter-charges, so that each faction is accusing the others. Already these murders are straining the city to breaking point. If they are succeeding in carrying out this evil plan, Bombay will explode . . .'

His words echoed Da Souza's earlier fears. I wondered what Dad, and the policemen, would make of their strange ally.

I rose. 'I must be getting back.'

Hussein chugged to a halt outside the Taj Mahal hotel and I got down.

'I'm afraid I'll have to owe you the fare,' I said. 'I'll pay you tomorrow.'

'Do not worry. Strictly speaking, motorised

rickshaws are not allowed in city centre,' said Hussein. 'You are telling your father and friends of danger?'

'I'll tell them,' I promised.

'Good!' said Hussein. 'We must all meet tomorrow at the temple as arranged.'

He chugged away.

It was almost dawn by now. I went into the deserted foyer of the hotel, only to find a scandalised hotel security man barring my way. I caught a glimpse of my dirty, ragged form in a hotel mirror and realised why.

'It's all right,' I said wearily. 'I may not look it but I'm a guest here. Matthew Stirling. Is my father awake?'

He insisted on escorting me to Dad's room. He rapped on the door and Dad opened at once.

'Professor Stirling, there is a boy here . . .'

Dad thrust him aside and grabbed hold of me in a bear hug.

'Matthew! Where on earth . . . ? I've been worried sick . . .'

'It's a bit of a long story, Dad,' I said, and fainted dead away.

*Chapter Ten*

# REUNION

It wasn't much of a faint really – I was ashamed of myself afterwards. But it had been a long night, with not much food – street snacks aside – no sleep, and a hell of a lot of nervous tension.

I was OK as soon as Dad got me inside and sitting down. I tried to tell him what had been happening, but he wouldn't listen. Not until I'd had a hot bath, got into pyjamas and dressing-gown, had a hot drink, something to eat and a thorough examination by the hotel doctor, who said I was physically and emotionally exhausted, but basically OK.

Only then did Dad let me tell my story.

When I'd got as far as the kidnapping he said, 'We were all frantic with worry. Da Souza's been dispatching police squads all over Bombay. . .' He jumped up. 'I must tell him you're back.'

He put through a quick call to Da Souza, who was still very much awake at police HQ. Da Souza insisted on coming round at once. Dad tried to put him off till later but he wouldn't have it.

'That producer chap Balin was frantic,' said Dad when he sat down again. 'He just wouldn't stop apologising. He fired half his security force for failing to stop the kidnapping.'

'Don't be too sorry for Mr Balin,' I said. 'I'm pretty certain he arranged the whole thing.'

'But his men tried to save you – I saw them,' protested Dad.

'His men *pretended* to try and save me,' I said. 'That big bodyguard, Jalil, fell down under a punch he could hardly have felt. Then he waved his arms about, being careful not to really hurt anyone. The others were doing the same. When those gangsters hauled me off, his men got in the way of the police.'

'But why should he go to such lengths?'

'He needed to kidnap me, to find out how much I knew and to put pressure on you and the police. But he knew that you knew where I was – I'd told him about the note I left for you. If I disappeared at the cinema, he'd be under suspicion. So he kept me at the cinema to give him time to arrange for some hired gangsters to kidnap me *in front of you* while his men faked trying to stop them. That way he was in the clear.'

'Why did he want to kidnap you at all?'

'Because he's behind all these murders,' I said.

I told him the rest of the story – my trip to the seaside, my rescue by Hussein, and our visit to the temple.

'The man behind the wheel of the limo looked familiar, and I suddenly realised it was Jalil, Balin's bodyguard. The big man in the temple had to be Balin himself.'

Dad sat silent for a moment, considering my story. 'You say there's some kind of paranormal force behind all this?'

I nodded. 'Not only that, it's one we've met before.'

'Where?'

'In Chile at the Inca temple in Machu Picchu.'

Some time ago we'd gone to Chile, to investigate a rebellion being stirred up by some paranormal force. We'd discovered that an alien entity had taken up residence in an Inca temple. It was using human pawns to cause a bloody rebellion – apparently for the sheer love of cruelty and bloodshed.

'But surely that – *thing*, whatever it was, was destroyed,' insisted Dad.

'Apparently not. Instead it's just – relocated.'

'What makes you so sure it's the same?'

'It feels the same. And it's using exactly the same

technique – embedding itself in some potentially violent part of human culture, and using it to cause mayhem and bloodshed, just for the fun of it!'

'You're sure it wasn't some kind of clever illusion?'

Before I could answer there was a knock at the door. Da Souza had arrived, and I had to tell the whole story again.

He listened intently, without comment.

When I'd finished he asked, 'And the supernatural element of your story, Matthew. You're certain about that?'

'I can only tell you what I saw.'

'It could not have been a delusion, some kind of hypnotism – like our famous Indian rope trick?'

You too! I thought wearily. Out loud I said, 'No. It was real.'

Da Souza sighed, not convinced. 'Well, we must deal with it as best we can.' He paused for a moment. 'And Mr Balin, what are his motives?'

'According to Hussein's source, Balin's more than a film producer. That's just his front. Really he's chief Don of your Mumbai Mafia. He's succeeded in uniting most of the gangs, and if the civic government breaks down in disorder they plan to take over. The gangs will run the city.'

'That wouldn't be much of a change,' said Da

Souza. 'They're practically doing it already. Maybe if they took over completely they'd do a better job – they could hardly do worse than the present lot.' He saw Dad's astonished face and smiled. 'Don't worry, professor. Whatever I think of our politicians, I'm still a policeman and I shall do my duty.' He turned to me. 'One piece of evidence supports your story, Matthew. We managed to identify the assassin killed in the garden. He was an aspiring young actor, no criminal record at all.'

I nodded. A film producer like Balin would have an endless supply of such people under his influence.

He rose. 'I must go, there are many arrangements to make. Congratulations on your escape, Matthew. You should get some sleep.'

Dad and I went to bed in the small hours, and didn't wake until well past noon. After lunch we joined Inspector Da Souza, who was busy with arrangements for the big raid. It was to be a full-scale affair with plenty of police and army manpower. Da Souza was taking no chances. When everything was planned and prepared, there was nothing to do but wait . . .

It was past midnight and we were all waiting in ambush. The area around the temple was ringed with police and soldiers. Balin was being watched, and instructions had been given that he, and any companions, should be allowed to reach the ruined building above the temple without any trouble.

Da Souza was at the head of the group with Hussein to act as guide. Dad and I were with him, and Lieutenant Mohan was close by with his troops.

Hussein had told Da Souza the location of the entrances to the temple and armed men had been posted outside each one. Their instructions were not to venture inside, but to stop anyone from escaping.

Hussein said all the tunnel entrances were booby-trapped except the main one that the blasphemers used themselves, which was always heavily guarded.

We heard the distant sound of engines. It grew louder and louder still. Not one but two stretch limos drove into the open space. They stopped and Balin got out of the first and Jalil out of the second.

They opened the passenger doors and a dozen white-clad young men poured out of each car. They must have been packed in like sardines. Without speaking they formed themselves into an orderly column and Balin led them away.

Jalil stayed behind, guarding the cars.

'Quickly,' whispered Hussein a few minutes later. 'Else a man is dying for each one of them.'

Silently police and troops surged forward, mopping up the astonished Jalil on the way. He was really fighting this time, not faking it, and it took four soldiers to subdue him. Finally he was handcuffed and gagged and tossed in the back of his own limo.

Hussein led us some distance through the ruins until we reached another, larger gap in the rubble. A group of guards like the ones we'd seen in the temple, armed like them with machine-pistols, stood lounging around. They didn't look particularly alert, and seemed to be expecting no trouble.

'There will be more inside,' warned Hussein. 'We must make no noise or the blasphemers will escape.'

Da Souza turned and beckoned, and Lieutenant Mohan appeared out of the darkness. There was another officer with him, a slim, dark man in black combat fatigues.

Da Souza whispered instructions and the slim man disappeared into the darkness. He returned minutes later with a squad of black-clad soldiers.

I turned to Mohan. 'How will they manage?' I whispered. 'If anyone so much as fires a shot Balin's lot will be warned.'

'Watch,' said Mohan quietly. 'These are top-class Indian commandos, damn fine fellows.'

The commandos crept stealthily forwards, then

overwhelmed the guards in a fierce silent rush. I saw a guard, more alert than the others, raise his machine-pistol to fire. There was a series of low popping sounds and he dropped. There was a brief silent struggle and the other guards dropped one by one.

'Silenced machine-guns,' explained Mohan. 'No noise!'

In a matter of minutes the guards were all killed or captured, and we all moved forward, commandos in the lead. The gap in the rubble led to another tunnel, far larger than the one we'd used earlier. It was wider, refreshingly free of rats and slime, and lit by blazing torches set into the walls.

Suddenly more guards rushed from a side tunnel, taking us by surprise. The commandos reacted instantly, dealing with them in the same deadly silence. The silenced machine-guns popped, and the guards fell.

Dad, Da Souza and I held back, leaving the fighting to the commandos.

All at once a frightened and confused guard swung round on us, raising his machine-pistol to mow us down. At this range he couldn't miss . . .

Something flicked round his neck, his body arched backwards, there was an all-too-familiar crack and he fell.

Behind him I saw Hussein tucking his *rumal* back into his sash.

With all the guards dead or surrendered the attack party moved on.

We turned a corner and came to an ornately-carved temple entrance. There were guards here too, but this time they were the ones to be surprised. The commandos' silenced machine-guns popped, and the guards fell one by one.

We moved silently towards the entrance.

It led us not to the balcony, but to a shadowy area at the back of the temple.

Torches flickered around the altar and Balin's assassins stood grouped before it. Balin himself stood in front of them. He raised his hands as if about to perform an incantation – but the crisp voice of Da Souza stopped him.

'That will do, Mr Balin. There will be no killings tonight.'

Commandos flooded into the temple and bustled Mr Balin and his disciples away down the tunnel, now suddenly brightly lit with big army lamps.

Da Souza turned to us with a smile of satisfaction. 'So – that is that!' He looked around the temple. 'And no demons, Matthew! I think they must have rigged up some illusion to impress their disciples. What our film people call a special effect – Balin is in the business, remember. We shall find it later, no doubt.'

He followed his men down the tunnel.

Now only Dad, Hussein and I remained in the temple.

'A very efficient operation,' said Dad approvingly. 'And as Inspector Da Souza said, no spooks, Matthew! Come along.'

He turned and followed Da Souza.

Hussein and I looked at each other for a moment.

'So, *sahib*, it is over,' said Hussein. 'The blasphemers have been destroyed and the honour of Kali is saved.'

Somehow reluctant to leave, we stood for a moment, gazing at the altar with the great statue of Kali behind it.

It was a moment too long.

The air before the altar suddenly *blurred* and a cold wind blew through the temple, extinguishing most of the torches.

Slowly the giant snake materialised in the gloom.

It reared high before us, weaving hypnotically, eyes gleaming.

A voice inside my head said, *'Come to me.'*

Helplessly I moved forward. Hussein came with me, compelled by the same terrible force.

The voice in my head spoke again.

*'Once before, you interfered with my amusements. I sensed your presence here, and reached out to you in your dreams. I shall have my revenge now. In time I shall find other human servants in other places, but you shall die.'*

Just as in my dream, the great head reared high above me, the giant fangs dripped blood . . .

I heard Hussein's voice beside me. 'Kali! O Kali!' A stream of rapid Hindi poured from his mouth, a prayer to the goddess.

I desperately wanted to join in, but I couldn't. I wasn't a follower of Hussein's strange and terrible religion, nor did I know the appropriate prayers.

All I could do was join the force of my will to Hussein's plea.

I invented a sort of prayer of my own, shouting out loud and projecting it with all my mental force.

'Please, Kali, hear the prayer of Hussein, your servant. He has risked everything for you. Don't abandon him now in the hour of danger! Don't let this evil force, this alien who has blasphemed your temple, destroy us!'

I heard the sound of Hussein's voice, rising and falling in a rapid, urgent chant. In our different ways we were both asking Kali for help.

The goddess heard. The statue of Kali came alive.

The eyes of the goddess glowed red, her many arms flailed angrily. She glared fiercely at us, her whole body surrounded by baleful radiance.

Sensing the presence of an older and more powerful force, the great snake swung round and reared menacingly above the statue.

A beam of light flashed from Kali's eyes, enveloping the great snake in flames. The monster gave a terrible, high-pitched scream and disintegrated into a pool of evil-smelling slime.

I turned to see if Hussein was all right and found him kneeling, hands raised in worship before the glowing statue, his face alight with ecstasy.

'Kali! O Kali!' he sobbed – and pitched forwards face-down.

I knelt beside him. 'Hussein!'

Summoned by the snake's dying scream, Dad, Da Souza, Mohan and an assortment of police and soldiers came running back into the temple.

'What happened?' asked Da Souza.

I looked up. 'The snake came. Hussein prayed to Kali for help – we both did, I suppose – and Kali came and destroyed the snake.'

He nodded, this time accepting what I'd said without question.

Dad knelt beside me and examined Hussein. 'Dead,' he said briefly. 'Heart stopped.'

We both rose. I looked at the statue. The glow had faded and it was just a statue again.

'Why?' I asked. 'He was her lifelong servant, and she answered his prayer. Why did she have to destroy him? And why not me as well?'

'Kali is a cruel goddess,' said Da Souza. 'Cruel and capricious. She must have her sacrifice, and Hussein was chosen, as you were spared, on Kali's whim.' He looked down at Hussein's body and sighed. 'Perhaps it was for the best. He died in her service. And considering all he's done for us – I'd hate to have had to investigate his past!'

Next day Dad and I both decided we'd had enough of Bombay, at least for the time being. Dad wrote a polite note to his computer boffin saying how sorry he was to have missed him, and booked us a nice restful holiday in Goa.

Da Souza came to the Taj Mahal hotel to say good-bye.

We stood outside the entrance as porters loaded our luggage into the taxi. It struck me that the busy scene stood for all Bombay – from the luxury hotel to the beggars around the Gateway of India.

'Goodbye,' said Da Souza. 'Thanks for all you've done for us.'

'I don't feel we did much,' I said. 'It was all Hussein – Hussein and Kali!'

'You both played your part,' he said. 'Especially you, Matthew. If you hadn't made that illicit trip to the cinema we might never have caught Balin.' He turned and looked at the cheerful seething crowd clustering around the Gateway of India.

It was a fine, sunny morning, and the multi-coloured bobbing balloons gave the harbour-front a festive air. Sunlight glinted on the waves.

'It's always been a struggle to survive in Bombay,' said Da Souza. 'It'll be years before most of these people have safe, secure lives. But they don't give up the fight. And at least they won't be making things worse by killing each other, just so some rich, fat crook can get richer and fatter. That's something to have achieved, isn't it?'

We all shook hands.

Then Dad and I climbed into our taxi and headed for the airport.